THE
DWARF-WIZARD
OF
UXMAL

THE DWARF-WIZARD OF
UXMAL

TOLD BY SUSAN HAND SHETTERLY
ILLUSTRATED BY ROBERT SHETTERLY

ATHENEUM 1990 NEW YORK

To Birdie and Pop
for their kindness and encouragement

Our thanks to Janet and George Cobb of Tikul,
Yucatan, who read the text for us and shared their wealth
of knowledge about their adopted homeland.

Text copyright © 1990 by Susan Hand Shetterly
Illustrations copyright © 1990 by Robert Shetterly

All rights reserved.
Atheneum
Macmillan Publishing Company
866 Third Avenue, New York, NY 10022
Collier Macmillan Canada, Inc.
First Edition
Printed in Hong Kong

Library of Congress Cataloging-in-Publication Data
Shetterly, Susan Hand.
The dwarf-wizard of Uxmal/retold by Susan Shetterly;
illustrated by Robert Shetterly.   p.   cm.
Summary: With the magical aid of the old woman who hatched him
from an egg, the diminutive Tol proves himself greater than the
ruler of the city of Uxmal and takes his place as leader of the
people.
ISBN 0-689-31455-8
1. Uxmal Site (Mexico)—Juvenile literature.   2. Legends—Mexico—
Yucatán (State)—Juvenile literature.   [1. Mayas—Legends.
2. Indians of Mexico—Yucatán (State)—Legends.]   I. Shetterly,
Robert, ill.   II. Title.
F1435.1.U7S53   1990
398.2′0972′65—dc20
[E]   89-32864   CIP   AC

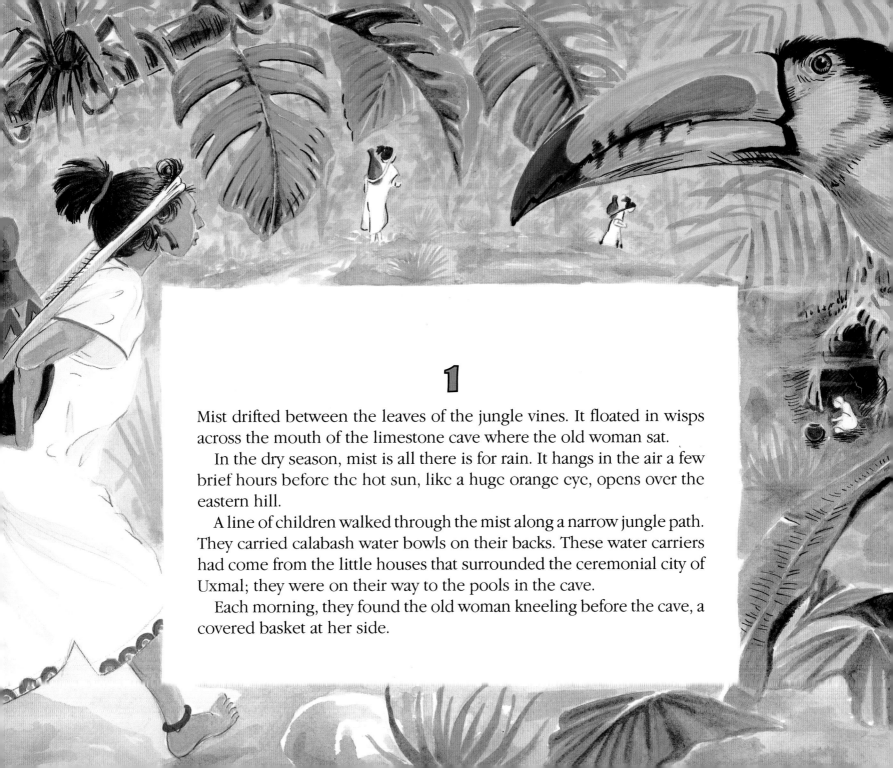

1

Mist drifted between the leaves of the jungle vines. It floated in wisps across the mouth of the limestone cave where the old woman sat.

In the dry season, mist is all there is for rain. It hangs in the air a few brief hours before the hot sun, like a huge orange eye, opens over the eastern hill.

A line of children walked through the mist along a narrow jungle path. They carried calabash water bowls on their backs. These water carriers had come from the little houses that surrounded the ceremonial city of Uxmal; they were on their way to the pools in the cave.

Each morning, they found the old woman kneeling before the cave, a covered basket at her side.

She held out her hand. In a voice as dry as corn husks in the wind, she cried, "An egg! Give me an egg and I will show you Tzab-Can!" From the basket they would hear a muffled noise, like raindrops hitting the parched jungle leaves.

"We don't want to see him," some of the water carriers grumbled.

"Listen!" The old woman tilted her head. "He sings with his tail!" She wheezed an old-bird laugh.

Then, as they always did, the first water carrier slowly drew an egg from her pocket and dropped it into the old woman's shiny palm. The children crowded forward as the old woman whispered something to the basket.

A hard, mean rattle rose out of it. The old woman flipped up the lid, and a black tongue darted over the basket's rim.

"It's Tzab-Can!" the children screamed, and jumped back. But they didn't let slip their calabash bowls.

The old woman squawked in glee. She slammed down the lid and turned to the children, smiling her wrinkly smile. "You see," she cackled, "how he waits for you."

The children hurried to the cave and climbed down the ladder that led to the shallow pools where chachalacas and ground doves came to drink in the dry season, and they filled their bowls.

Every morning, when they climbed out, the old woman had disappeared, and so had the mist.

Before they reached their dooryards, they could hear the conch-shell trumpets sounding from the top of the Governor's Palace to announce the rising sun. And they could see through the tops of the trees to the Great Pyramid, where priests rushed nimbly over the steps, the plumes of their headdresses rippling as they ran.

The water carriers did not know it, but the old woman's hut stood in the deep jungle not far from their own. Sometimes she fed the egg they had given her to her snake. Sometimes she cooked it and ate it herself. But once, because she had always wanted a child, she wrapped an egg in one of her dresses, which are called huipils, and set it on a smooth white stone on the floor. Then she knelt and prayed to her gods, and waited for the egg to hatch.

The next morning, the children did not find her at the cave.

"Tzab-Can bit her," they said. But that was not true.

When the sun went down, Tzab-Can carefully climbed to the top of the huipil and curled himself around it to keep the egg safe all night as the old woman prayed.

Day after day, the dry season cracked the land and turned the soil to dust. The old woman sat in front of the covered egg as the sun burned down on the roof of her hut. At mid-day it grew so hot that even the snake

could hardly move. He slumped in a heap on the floor.

But one evening, the old woman heard a noise, as if thousands of mice were rushing over the roof thatch. She hadn't heard that sound in a long time.

The rains had come.

When the snake, who was lying by the doorway, felt the cool drops splashing on his skin, he rippled off into the jungle.

Suddenly, the huipil moved. A shriek, like the cry of a tiny jungle bird, burst from it. The old woman lifted a sleeve of the huipil, and there stood a little boy.

"My prayers are answered!" the old woman cried. He was the finest little boy she had ever seen.

She fed him wild honey from the hives of the stingless Mayan bees, and corn tortillas that she cooked on a stone over the open fire. She fed him beans and chayote squash and papayas that she harvested from her milpa plot. But he grew no taller than the little jungle deer. He just grew older.

The boy saw the children of Uxmal as they walked the jungle path to the cave. He would hide behind the trunk of a ceiba tree and watch them laughing together as they lugged their calabash bowls. He saw that they did not look the same as he did. And he was afraid of them.

The boy played with his friend the snake during the dry seasons. When the rains fell, he and the old woman worked until dark in the milpa.

On the day of his fifteenth year, the old woman spoke gently to him. "My son, you are Tol, the dwarf-wizard. One day you shall rule the great city of Uxmal."

"But I like it here," he whimpered. "I like it with Tzab-Can and you!" He ran into the hut and wrapped himself up in his hammock and turned his back on her.

After a time the old woman spoke to him again. "Tomorrow you will go to the governor. I will tell you what to say."

That night Tol could not sleep. He watched the lamp that she had set in the center of the floor. Its flame flickered in the darkness.

A small, round owl landed on his hammock strings. It leaned forward.

"Don't be frightened!" the owl whistled in his ear.

The bird flew, brushing across his face. It snuffed the flame of the lamp as it passed. Tol sighed a deep sigh. He curled into his hammock and fell asleep.

"Tell the governor," the old woman said, holding on to Tol's thin shoulders and looking sternly into his eyes, "that you have come to lead the people. That you are the dwarf-wizard. He will understand."

Tol raised his hands and nervously tried to press the strands of his hair down flat. But they popped up again, like the feathers on the head of a hawk eagle.

Dutifully, he marched alone down the path to the city. The old woman watched him go.

Groove-billed anis scattered silently ahead of him, drifting off the branches of the flowering yellow elder trees. As he reached the Governor's Palace, an iguana skittered over the steps and flipped down a hole. Tol began to climb. Up he went until he stood on the wide stone terrace that overlooked the Puuc hills. Before him, dressed in jaguar skins and holding spears made of obsidian, stood five broad-chested guards. They wore shark teeth and jaguar claws and brightly colored beads in ropes around their necks. Toucan feathers glistened in their hair. They looked down at Tol and they laughed.

"Get away, mosquito!" one of the guards bellowed.

"I am not a mosquito," retorted Tol, his feelings stung. "Kindly tell the governor the dwarf-wizard is here."

Briefly, Tol thought that the guards looked frightened. But they began to laugh again. And as they laughed, their feathers trembled and their shark teeth chattered and the long, curved claws rattled against the beads.

Tol walked past them into the palace, where the governor sat on his two-headed jaguar throne. The governor was asleep. He was snoring. A fly had landed on his nose and was casually cleaning its wings.

Tol kneeled down and picked up a fan that lay by the throne. Aiming carefully, he smashed it on the foolish fly.

"Ayye! Yayee! Yayee!" yelled the governor, leaping from the throne as the guards rushed through the doorway.

"Who is this creature?" the governor roared.

"I am the dwarf-wizard," Tol stuttered, as the guards held him by the arms. The room became silent.

"You are what?"

"The dwarf-wizard."

"I doubt it," growled the governor, looking down at Tol. "It is written in the *Book of Prophesy* that the dwarf-wizard is stronger than twenty men. You are no stronger than that fly." He pointed to the squashed fly lying in the corner of the room.

"Go home. Go back to your milpa and let me sleep."

"I can lift a rock," Tol insisted.

"And I can lift ten rocks at once—one on each finger of my hands," snarled the governor. "Go away before I heave you into the hills."

"Please, Governor," Tol persisted, although he thought he might faint with fear, "challenge me to a test of strength."

The governor leaned down until his face was no more than a few inches from the face of Tol. His mouth hung open in disbelief.

"Little man," he rasped, "you come here tomorrow when the sun begins to lift above that temple over there," and he waved his arm to the east. "We will have done with you then."

The governor sank back against his throne. "Take him away," he gestured. And his eyes closed.

"You will win, Tol." The old woman chortled gleefully. But Tol hardly heard her. He felt so weak he could barely lift a tortilla to his mouth. The snake coiled around his leg, comfortingly.

"Tomorrow you must let the governor take hold of every object first," the old woman told him as she lighted the lamp and set it on the floor. "And I will cook you a special tortilla. Use it in case of danger."

Again Tol lay awake in the night until a ringtail cat leaped to the hammock strings. Startled, he turned and saw its black eyes reflecting the lamp's yellow glow.

"Don't be frightened," the cat whispered, touching its wet nose to Tol's cheek. Then it was gone, across the floor and through the door. Its tail flicked out the burning wick as it ran.

"So, little cockroach," boomed the governor, "you think you are stronger than I!"

"Yes, sir," Tol gasped. The governor was dressed in a vest of quilted armor. Around his bulging calves he wore deerskin garters, and at his stomach hung a belt made from the skins of coralita snakes. The green tail feathers of the resplendent quetzal glittered in his headdress as the

first rays of the sun glanced off the top of the Great Pyramid.

Four trumpeters stood at the corners of the terrace and blew on their conch shells to announce the contest. But a crowd had already gathered. The water carriers were there, and the warriors, the milpa farmers, the mothers with babies in their arms, and the old men leaning on chicle-tree canes.

Soldiers forced a path as the governor made his way down the steps. Tol followed. They strode into the center of the ball court. People tittered and jeered. "Hey, you," someone yelled at Tol. "You can hardly lift your own feet."

Through the archway of the Quadrangle a man appeared pulling a javelina sow—the most enormous sow Tol had ever seen. The man held her by a piece of sisal rope tied to one of her fat back legs. As he yanked, the sow squealed and snapped her sharp yellow teeth. Panting and exhausted, he dragged her before the governor.

"The oldest, biggest sow in all Mayab, sir—and the meanest."

The governor laughed. His laughter rumbled the length of the ball court like thunder at the end of the dry season. He leaned down, grabbed the animal around her belly, and heaved her, thrashing, into the air. Then he dropped her in front of Tol. Fury burned in her wicked, red eyes.

Tol spoke to her in a low voice. "I don't like this, either," he said. The sow continued to glare at him. But he thought he saw her expression soften. He put his skinny arms around her belly and began to lift. To his surprise, she weighed no more than a leaf. And she seemed to enjoy the ride. In one arm, he lifted her even higher, then set her on his finger, where she found that she could balance by a delicate, pointed hoof. The people in the crowd held their breath. The governor howled.

He rushed to a limestone block into which carvers were chiseling an outline of his face. He pushed them roughly aside and hurled himself at

the stone. He could bring it an inch off the ground. Satisfied, he dropped it, slapped the rock dust from his hands, and turned to Tol, who was letting the sow pirouette on his palm.

Tol put her down gently and walked uneasily to the stone. He lifted. To his amazement, it weighed no more than a pebble. He tossed it from one hand to the other. Then the sow leaped into the air and Tol juggled them both, throwing them high as the crowd whooped its delight.

The governor rushed to an old man and snatched away his chicle-tree cane. Then he ran at Tol. Quickly, Tol set the sow and the stone on the ground. He yanked the special tortilla from his belt and slapped it onto his head. The cane whacked down. It shattered into hundreds of pieces. But Tol hardly felt the blow.

Slowly, as if he were losing air, the governor fainted. He sank to the ground. His guards gathered around, lifted him, and carried him up the palace steps. The people turned away from Tol. In silence, they followed the guards and the limp governor.

Tol slipped back into the jungle. He found the path to his home. Once he thought he heard footsteps behind him and, turning, saw that the javelina had followed. He whistled softly to her, and they walked on together, hardly making a sound.

3

Tol and the old woman husked corn in the milpa as the shrill songs of the cicadas vibrated in their ears. Tol beat at the dry corn with a pole until the hard kernels popped free from the cobs and dropped to the ground, where the old woman scooped them up and poured them into baskets.

They burned the jungle plot for the new-year planting. Smoke from their fires rose in gray clouds to cover the sun. When the burning was done, Tol and the old woman rested in the shade of a cotton tree and waited for the rains. But no rain fell. Tzab-Can slept curled in the dust in Tol's shadow. The javelina rooted in the milpa after the last few kernels of corn.

Every year they waited for the rains. And always, after they had almost given up hope, there would be a sudden gust. The sky would darken. The sun would disappear. And drops would plunge straight from the sky.

This year the rains were late. The long drought distressed Tol. He was tired of the endless days of heat. But his heart was light. The old woman had not mentioned the governor nor the city of Uxmal again.

One day, the santeja, a deep hole in the rocks where the old woman fetched water, and where the jungle animals came to drink, went dry. The next day, the cave where the water carriers dipped their calabash bowls held only enough to fill one bowl. Tol listened to the toh birds. "Kawock," they moaned, from dawn to dusk.

That night, the old woman spoke. "You must go to the governor," she said. "You must tell him if he does not call in the rains for his people and for all the creatures of the jungle, you will."

"Ha!" cried Tol, without mirth. "How can I call in the rains when even the javelina won't listen to me—when even Tzab-Can disobeys?"

"You will see. You will see."

Once again, before sleep, the old woman lighted the lamp and placed it on the dirt floor of the hut.

Tol lay in his hammock. He stared at the ceiling. A young fruit bat shouldered its way through the thatch and dropped into the still air of the room. As it circled, Tol could see its thick fur, and its big, dark eyes. The bat dipped low and put out the light.

"Don't worry, Tol!" it squeaked as it flew away.

"How are you going to talk to the Chac, the Rain God?" shouted the governor, spraying Tol in the face. "I am the only one who talks to the Chac...." But his words trailed off. He gazed out the archway, past the terrace, to the city below. The people, in their clean white clothes, holding their water gourds, sat quietly around a well. There was only enough in the wells of Uxmal for half a gourdful for each family each day. The water the guard drew up was warm and mud streaked.

"I must go tonight to speak from the cave of Loltun. The Chac will hear me there. He will give us some rain." The governor licked his cracked lips. He cleared his throat.

"Now be gone," he said with a sigh.

Tol ordered the javelina to stay by the hut. She followed him, anyway, through the jungle to the white highway that led out of Uxmal, through the arch of Labna, to the great, deep cave of Loltun.

It was growing dark. Up ahead marched the governor's retinue. As the night fell, soldiers lighted torches that cast eerie shadows against the trees. Tol hurried in the moonlight that shone off the highway. The javelina trotted cheerfully behind.

When they came to the mouth of the cave, the guards took hold of the governor and hoisted him out of his ceremonial hammock. One by one

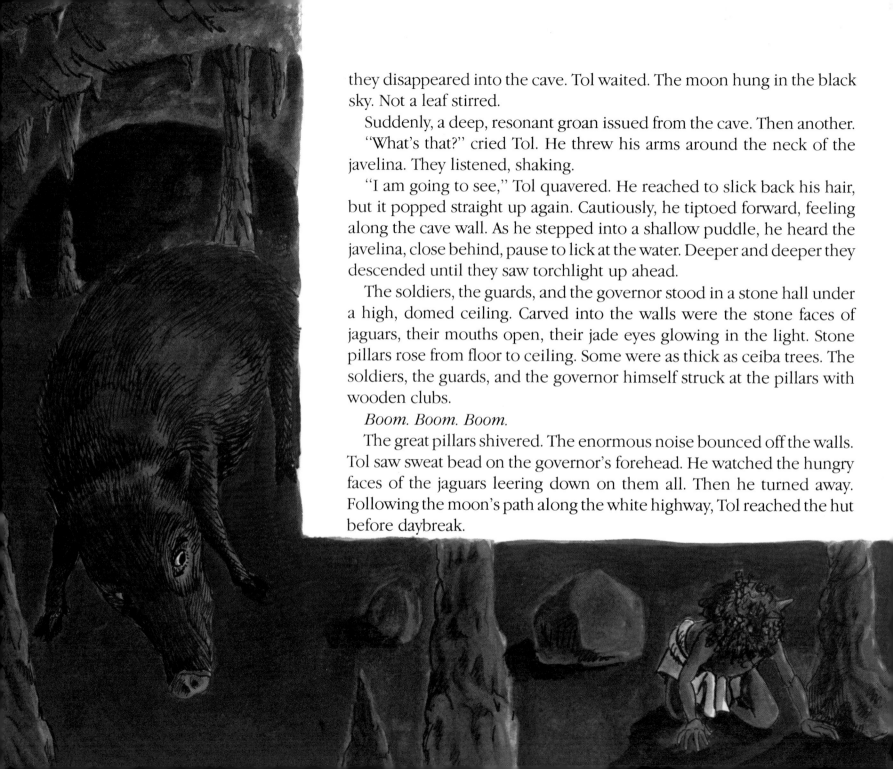

they disappeared into the cave. Tol waited. The moon hung in the black sky. Not a leaf stirred.

Suddenly, a deep, resonant groan issued from the cave. Then another.

"What's that?" cried Tol. He threw his arms around the neck of the javelina. They listened, shaking.

"I am going to see," Tol quavered. He reached to slick back his hair, but it popped straight up again. Cautiously, he tiptoed forward, feeling along the cave wall. As he stepped into a shallow puddle, he heard the javelina, close behind, pause to lick at the water. Deeper and deeper they descended until they saw torchlight up ahead.

The soldiers, the guards, and the governor stood in a stone hall under a high, domed ceiling. Carved into the walls were the stone faces of jaguars, their mouths open, their jade eyes glowing in the light. Stone pillars rose from floor to ceiling. Some were as thick as ceiba trees. The soldiers, the guards, and the governor himself struck at the pillars with wooden clubs.

Boom. Boom. Boom.

The great pillars shivered. The enormous noise bounced off the walls. Tol saw sweat bead on the governor's forehead. He watched the hungry faces of the jaguars leering down on them all. Then he turned away. Following the moon's path along the white highway, Tol reached the hut before daybreak.

But no rain fell.

The toh birds sat on the branches of the jungle trees. "Kawock," they complained. One afternoon, Tzab-Can stirred in Tol's shadow. He rattled his tail, turned his head toward the uncut jungle, and flicked his thin, black tongue. Gradually, he uncoiled and slipped away. Tol hurried after.

Before long, Tzab-Can drew back. They had come to a hole in the jungle floor. Its sides were white and smooth; it was an entrance to a small cave.

Tol followed Tzab-Can. They climbed into the soft, powdery brightness. Almost immediately, the cave ended at a chalky room. Asleep on the floor, their eyes closed, lay forty tortoises. Their easy breathing filled the cave chamber like a wind.

"Why did you bring me here, Tzab-Can?" Tol whispered. But the snake curled in front of the tortoises and dropped his head across his coils. Tol sat down to wait.

Lulled by the sleeping tortoises and the airy coolness of the cave, Tol's head nodded.

When he awoke, Tol found that Tzab-Can was still lying beside him. The tortoises still slept on the white floor. For a reason he could not afterward recall, he began talking solemnly to the sleeping tortoises.

"My friends," he said, "the rains have not come."

Tol saw the largest tortoise at the back of the chamber raise its head. Tol stared. The neck that stretched from under the shell looked like an old piece of rope. A small head wobbled like a knot at the end of it. But the eyes that gazed at him seemed kind and immeasurably sad.

"Because no rain has fallen," Tol continued, "the lizard trembles." Two more tortoises raised their heads.

"And the toh bird calls...." Five tortoises stirred.

"The leaves on the monkey tree wither and fall...." Ten tortoises looked up.

"And the thirsty children of Uxmal are crying for water!" Tol shouted as twenty-two tortoises opened their eyes.

Rhythmically, they swung their heads from side to side. Their beaks fell open and they growled. As they trod, growling, past Tzab-Can and Tol, their claws scraped at the soft limestone. Single file, they marched out of the cave. Tol noticed that big tears had welled up in their eyes.

He scrambled after them.

The tortoises, as old as the stones of Mayab, arranged themselves—with some difficulty—into a perfect circle. They swung their heads. Their growling filled the air.

But beyond the hills, Tol thought he could hear thunder as the tears of the tortoises coursed down their wrinkled faces.

Another rumble. All at once, the sky turned dark. Then the great Rain God, the Chac, pounded above the jungle trees. Tol lifted up his hands as drops splattered against his palms and to the ground.

4

Day after day, the rains fell. Tol planted the milpa. The corn seemed to sprout up right behind him in the warm, wet ground. The chayote squash vines uncoiled over the rust-colored soil like a nest of green snakes. And every day, someone from the city found an excuse to drop by.

Word had spread. The people believed that Tol possessed secret magic powers, that he could make his wishes known even to the Chac.

The children of Uxmal brought him gum to chew from the chicle trees. A farmer asked him to find a hive of the wild, stingless bees, and he did, with the help of the javelina, who adored the smell and the taste of honey.

Tol was happy. The old woman had not mentioned the day of the tortoises nor the governor. Tol thought he could live like this forever.

But early one evening, as frogs trilled and toads chirred, as Tol lay in his hammock, rocking lazily, and the old woman ground corn for the morning tortillas, a shadow fell across the doorway.

"Little one!" rumbled a familiar voice. The governor shouldered his way into the hut. He was alone.

"My people talk about you," he snarled. "I do not like what they say." Tol and the old woman skittered to their feet.

"What do they say, sir?" Tol's voice was hoarse with dread.

"Ha! Ha! A foolish thing! They are calling you the dwarf-wizard! But you see, my silly snail, you cannot be. In our *Book of Prophesy*, the dwarf-wizard will build a temple when he comes—and he'll build it in a day!"

The old woman's eyes narrowed. For an uncomfortable moment, she looked to Tol like one of the stone jaguars in the cave of Loltun.

"Governor—" Her voice was brittle.

"Old woman?"

"Tol will build this temple you speak of tonight." Tol grasped the hammock ropes to steady himself. His knees shook so violently he thought he might pitch forward.

"At sunrise," she continued, "it will throw its shadow down across your terrace."

The governor shrugged in disgust. "Your brains have been stripped by locusts, old woman. But I will wait until dawn." He turned at the doorway. "If this temple does not stand in the city of Uxmal by sunrise, you and the boy must pay."

5

Tol could not believe his eyes. Here it was, the last night of their lives, and the old woman was breaking off pieces of corn mush, shaping them into little bricks, and setting them by the fire to dry.

He hung in the doorway, looking out into the rainy night. He hardly noticed the sweet smell of the earth or the green smell of the new corn shoots. A tear ran down his cheek.

"Come and help me, Tol," crooned the old woman.

It was no use—this crazy old woman planned to go on playing with cornmeal until the governor's soldiers came for her. Because he didn't know what else to do, Tol knelt down at her side. Before long, he and the old woman had spread toy bricks all over the floor of the hut.

"Now, build a temple," she said. And he did. He shaped it like a pyramid, with smooth, inclined sides and steep stairs. At the top, he built a small house with a wide doorway. When he had finished, the old woman stood back and nodded.

"You have built a place fit for a king," she said.

He laughed. "And do you suppose *this* is what the governor expects? A tortilla castle no higher than my knees?" She did not answer, but sprinkled boiling water onto the structure and fanned it until it dried as hard as adobe.

The rain had stopped. A full moon shone in the night sky. Tol did as the old woman bade him. He carried the temple in a tumpline toward the city.

The jungle is never a safe place at night. Once the narrow, copper-colored eyes of a jaguar blinked in front of him. Tol stopped. He clenched a fist. He bellowed at the cat in a voice that shook the jungle leaves. The eyes blinked once more, then disappeared. Tol walked on.

At the city that slept in darkness, he set down the little temple. He was glad no one had seen him. He felt foolish putting a toy where a real building was supposed to be.

When Tol returned home at dawn, he found the old woman sitting in the doorway. Mist rose around her. Her huipil and her hair were as white as the mist. Her arms were as pale as spiderwebs. She looked like a ghost. But she gave him a radiant smile.

"You must return right away to Uxmal," she urged.

"Oh, no!" He groaned. But he knew that the governor would awaken soon. Perhaps, if he returned, the soldiers would not look for the old woman at the hut. After hugging her good-bye and scratching the javelina on the head, Tol turned around and followed the path back.

The javelina trotted after him.

"So, old friend," he said, "the governor will make stew of us both." They stepped from the jungle as the sun broke above the Puuc hills. Before them a great temple lifted its lofty, smooth sides to the sky.

Tol laughed in surprise. He sniffed. The air around the temple smelled just a tiny bit like corn cakes. Tol raced over to the steps. The javelina sprinted after him. They climbed. Just as they reached the house, sunlight splashed against the temple walls. Tol turned to see the Governor's Palace drowned in shadow.

"I am the dwarf-wizard after all!" he cried.

People came running. They waved. They shouted. Like an ancient, wounded iguana peering out of its hole, the governor leaned from his palace and looked up. He staggered out the doorway, climbed down the terrace, and limped through the ball court. He crawled up the castle steps, one slow foot after the other.

"Beetle," he wheezed, as he gained the top, "the city is yours." He slumped next to the javelina. "I didn't much like being governor, anyhow."

"Then," Tol said, "you shall be my captain of the guards—what do you say to that?"

Years passed. Throughout Mayab, Uxmal's reputation for the grace of its buildings, the goodness of its people, and its clever dwarf-wizard grew.

Official visitors to the temple startled briefly when they found a snake resting on the dwarf's feet or when they tripped over a javelina sprawled on the castle floor. Some of them puzzled at the great, fat guard who snored all day by the dwarf-wizard's door.

Little children, leaning out of their hammocks at night, sometimes spotted a queer, bent shape descend the castle steps. They watched it slip into the jungle and disappear.

Tol never forgot the old woman. At night, in the dark, he'd sit by the light of the flickering lamp. He spoke to her of the questions a ruler must answer, the decisions a ruler must make. And she listened, as still as the moon in the Mayab sky.